Hannah's New Boots

Celia Berridge

Cartwheel
·B·O·O·K·S· ™

Scholastic Inc.

New York Toronto London Auckland Sydney

Originally published in 1992 in the UK by André Deutsch Children's Books/Scholastic
Publications Ltd.

Text copyright © 1992 by Celia Berridge.
Illustrations copyright © 1992 by Celia Berridge.
All rights reserved. Published in the U.S.A. by Scholastic Inc.,
730 Broadway, New York, NY 10003, by arrangement with
Scholastic Publications Ltd.
CARTWHEEL BOOKS is a trademark of Scholastic Inc.

Library of Congress Cataloging-in-Publication Data

Berridge, Celia.
    Hannah's new boots/Celia Berridge.
    p. cm.
    Summary: A little girl is enthralled by her new red boots which go everywhere she goes.
    ISBN: 0-590-45888-4
    [1. Boots — Fiction.] I. Title.
PZ7.B45975Han 1992   92-14124
[E] — dc20   CIP
                                                                 AC

12 11 10 9 8 7 6 5 4 3 2 1   3 4 5 6 7 8/9

                    Printed in the U.S.A.   37

             First Scholastic printing, May 1993

Here comes Hannah in her new boots,
new boots,
bright red shiny boots,
new from the shop,
ker-flip, ker-flop.

Up and down the hallway — *squish, squash,*
squish, squash —
Hannah walks her new boots.
(What a funny feeling!)
Heel toe, heel toe, *glip-glop.*

Hannah takes her boots off — big tug,
heave-ho —
mails them in the trash can,
down among the garbage,
just to see.

Are they still inside it? Poke down,
right down.
Hannah knocks it over,
bottles, boots, and garbage, and
the top rolls free.

Here comes Hannah in her new boots,
red boots,
out into the garden
(now inside the blue top).
Out to play
(What a day!)
in the sun.

Climbing from the sand box — steep step,
big step —
Hannah takes a tumble,
(stumbles in the blue top).
Trips in her new boots —
not much fun!

Here sits Hannah with her boots on,
boots on,
sitting in the high chair,
eating up her noodles,
drinking from her cup, and
banging on the tray.

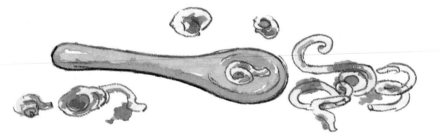

Hannah takes her toys out, big bear,
little bear,
blocks and trucks and plastic bricks,
paintbrushes and panda,
stuffs them in her new boots —
funny game to play!

There goes Pussy with her soft tail,
soft feet,
out through the cat door.
Hannah mails her new boots
out there, too.

"Look, it's started raining!" Hannah cries,
Hannah wails.
"I can't reach the handle;
Mama, bring my boots in!"
What a big to-do!

Daddy fills the bathtub — *splish, splash, splosh, splosh —*
Hannah makes the bubbles,
Mama gets the towel and
the boots stay dry.

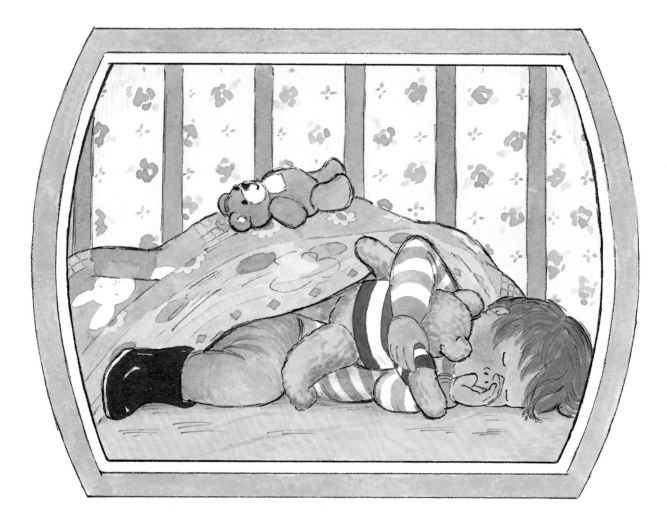

Here lies Hannah with her big bear,
little bear,
sleeping with her boots on,
new red boots on.
Good night, Hannah. Good-bye.